POSTLUDES

by
Matthew Burnside

KERNPUNKT PRESS

1st Printing: 2017

ISBN-13 978-0-9972924-2-8

KERNPUNKT Press
701 State Route 12B
Hamilton, New York 13346

www.kernpunktpress.com

ACKNOWLEDGEMENTS

"Cosmonauts/nots/knots" appeared in Ninth Letter; "Anti-Midnight in the Kingdom of Yes" + "Consequence of Splitting the Atom" both appeared in > kill author; "Sunken Dreamers' Almanac" appeared in Pear Noir!; "On the Benefits of a Lego Heart, Which Unlike Human Hearts Can Be Rebuilt Again and Again Knowing the Resilience of Their Delicate Construction Even as They're Being Smashed Against Something like a House or Tree Trunk or Even Your Daddy's Old Pickup Truck with the Missing Left Rearview Mirror and Faulty Cab Lights" appeared in Hobart; Portions of "Reliquary for the Trampled Underfoot" appeared in Contrary and The Dirty Napkin; "Escapology" appeared in NAP; "Passengers" appeared in Concho River Review with the alternate title "Dog Death Requiem"; "Rules to Win the Game" appeared in Zahir and Mary: A Journal of New Writing; "Oblivion's Fugue" appeared in the Stone Hobo and Revolution House; "Preludes" appeared in Prick of the Spindle; "Revival" appeared in Juked; In Search Of: A Sandbox Novel appeared in Best American Experimental Writing 2015; Totidem Verbis appeared in Permafrost

"The story ends. It was written for several reasons. Nine of them are secrets. The tenth is that one should never cease considering human love, which remains as grisly and golden as ever, no matter what is tattooed upon the warm tympanic page."

☐ Donald Barthelme

POSTLUDE ONE

There is the story of the writer trapped in his beginnings, writing this sentence even now but unable to pull the trigger, to bleed forward into a bigger world. The story of perfection oblivious of beauty in absence of headlights, of unfolding a road one inky inch at a time, delighting in a buffet of fog. The story of two feet grafted to the precipice of a page, a mouth full of mermaids, unable to chew loose through a velvet blowtorch. The story of a scab encased in holes, an escalator made of Jell-O, a zipper pinned to a skull projected on a portrait of paradise by a stationary carousel horse—of the raw countries of animals divisible by falling versus flight.

OBLIVION'S FUGUE

(Fifty-one things you'll never know, for better or worse...)

1. The night S went, it didn't hurt.

2. Exactly eleven years and three months after you called that kid with pockmarks and an oversized head *Freakzilla* in the third grade, he made his first cool million. When asked what he attributed his enormous success to, he cited all the years he was bullied by you.

3. Your first love never considered you her first love, just a warm body at a very difficult time in her life.

4. You were the only face your grandmother recognized in the room the night she died. The last memory that fluttered across her frail mind was of you both playing poker on a moonlit patio for pennies. She let you win every hand.

5. After buying lottery tickets for a quarter of your life, you quit because your son finally convinced you it was a waste of money. The very next week the winning numbers matched your wife's birthday, the same numbers you had played religiously for six years. The 5.6 million dollar payout wouldn't have made you any happier.

6. The Mexican who mows your lawn every other week speaks

perfect English. He nods and laughs when you address him in Spanish because he's shy and a bad conversationalist. He's never once been to Mexico.

7. The thousands of dollars spent on your liberal arts degree could've just as easily been spent on all the vacations you wish you had taken. The life experience would've been more valuable than the regurgitated ramblings of your burnt-out professors.

8. The man who robbed your house last Spring used the money he got from pawning your furniture to buy his son braces. You were the orthodontist who put them in. You considered it your finest work.

9. Your soft-spoken receptionist likes to dye her hair and dress up in leather on the weekends. She frequents death metal clubs and drops acid while experimenting with multiple partners in bathrooms and back alleys.

10. The marriage counselor you and your wife saw during that rocky patch has been divorced three times.

11. The people at the funeral home accidentally cremated your Aunt Jean when they mixed up their bodies. Fortunately, it was a closed casket funeral and nobody cared enough to view her.

12. All that pot you buried as a teenager in the backyard of your first house was later dug up by two brothers having a campout. As they threw it into the fire, they couldn't understand why they

were laughing so much. While raiding the house for Capri Suns and Captain Crunch and Pop Tarts, they stumbled upon their mother in bed with a man who wasn't their father. Years later, after the divorce, the boys would often smoke pot together in the backyard to escape their mutual feelings of inadequacy.

13. The reason your brother orders food for his wife any time you're at a new restaurant together has nothing to do with him wanting to appear a dominant husband. She cannot read the menu because she never learned to read. At night, they read picture books together in bed while he rubs her calloused feet.

14. The love you take is not necessarily equal to the love you make.

15. That elderly lady you ignored at the gas station who kept trying to get your attention only wanted your help working the gas pump. For forty years, her husband had been the one to put gas in the car. She had just come back from his funeral.

16. *Pixie* didn't die under the wheel of your father's truck like he told you she did. He simply lost sight of her in the garage one morning. He searched the neighborhood for six hours, finally slouched back through the front door to your mother a broken man, terminally ashamed and riddled with frostbite. He couldn't look her in the eyes. That night was the coldest night of the year. Rather than let you believe your dog froze to death, he made up a story.

17. Your mother dreamed of being a ballerina. She stopped dreaming

when she became pregnant with your brother. She never could get back in shape. She kept a pair of ragged ballet shoes at the top of her closet. Some days she would put them on and dance in front of a mirror. She was good enough to make it as a professional, had things been different.

18. That clown who gave your granddaughter a balloon at the circus is a manic depressive. He has a betta fish at home, a voluminous collection of comic books, and an ivy league education.

19. Though your Presbyterian preacher did go missing, it wasn't because he was guilty, as everyone in the congregation believed. He simply lost faith after his daughter Wimberley was murdered. He couldn't stand to lie about the Kingdom of Heaven anymore, or live across from the park where she once played, so he moved to Africa. Later, while watching a baby zebra being born - Wimberley's favorite animal - he would make his peace with God.

20. The reason your grandfather forbade you from playing guns in the house is because he shot a Japanese boy in the face during the war. He never told anybody, not even your grandmother. The bowl of goo you found in the garage was really just your plastic army men that he melted down in the microwave.

21. That strange baby carrot you found in your salad wasn't a carrot.

22. The fifty dollar bill you accidentally gave to that bum went towards the purchase of a secondhand suit and a haircut. At the

interview, he nervously hid his hands in his pockets when it dawned on him that he forgot to clip his margarine-colored fingernails. He got the job.

23. The cousin who never talks to anybody at all the family reunions lost her virginity to your favorite uncle Barry. It was not consensual.

24. The night you began to take form in your mother, your parents discussed getting a divorce while dining at a McDonalds. By the time the doctor was handing you off to your father, they had both forgotten they even had this conversation.

25. 3,002 is the number of times you have ignored your mother's phone calls. 10,101 is the number of times your son has ignored yours.

26. That wrong number last month wasn't a wrong number. The sister you never knew you had still can't conjure the right words to introduce herself.

27. Falling up the sky, waving to your smiling wife as she's swallowed by a pool of quicksand, the plink of your loose teeth as you struggle to catch them in a ceramic bowl are all recurring dreams you cannot remember having.

28. You would've lost both your legs in that car wreck had that truck driver not stopped to pull you out when he did. He is a registered sex offender who chose life on the road to keep his mind busy. Every

single day he wakes up and wrestles with temptation, and every night he thanks Jesus for the fortitude to have made it through another day without hurting anyone around him.

29. All the stories in the history of story (including this one) and all the songs in the history of song combined could not capture the strangeness, wonder, ecstasy, or terror of being alive as you and nobody else in the wingbeat of this moment. Chances are it will never happen again, so make it count.

30. Those black guys walking through the neighborhood about which you made the casually sarcastic remark: *Wonder what they'rreee up to?* were on their way to the library to recheck their books.

31. The patient with perfect teeth who insists on scheduling more frequent than routine cleanings is a kleptomaniac. Whenever you're not in the room, she sticks another toothbrush in her purse.

32. Your mother hasn't slept through a single night without taking a sleeping pill since your father's heart attack.

33. Emily Waltz wanted nothing more than to stick her tongue down your throat all throughout middle school. You didn't know her name but your brother did. She slept with him to get closer to you.

34. Your best friend regrets never telling you he's gay. His fiancée regrets the fact that he told her.

35. Because you missed that flight to Los Angeles, your seat was offered to a business man trying to make it back to his family in time for Thanksgiving. Because the left wing was faulty, the plane careened into a cornfield in Kansas, leaving no survivors. Because you missed your flight, you met your future wife at a Holiday Inn.

36. In your brother's eyes, you will never live down that time at summer camp that you fell asleep on a mound of fire ants and were made to strip while being hosed off in front of the girls' lodge.

37. The janitor at your old elementary school knows where the body of Wimberley Scot is. It's underneath the slide, where he buried it. Every time the recess bell rings, a bloodburst flash of giddiness passes over him and he can't help but snicker.

38. On the bus you rode to San Antonio, the young woman you sat by and had a conservation with appreciated the fact you didn't once look down her blouse. She was a sex worker trying to start her life over. You were the first man in two years who treated her like a person instead of a thing.

39. That lump beneath your armpit isn't benign. Your doctor never finished medical school.

40. Your son dragged a fire extinguisher to the backyard when he was seven because he had spent three weeks building a rocket to Hell out of cardboard and he was ready for the trial run. When someone from school told him his mother was going there for committing

suicide, he vowed to rescue her. The rocket did not achieve flight.

41. What matters most is not how well you walk through the fire but how far you walk after the flames have been extinguished.

42. Portia Macintosh never forgot that kiss under the bleachers on prom night. Three times over the years she has nearly sent you a message on Facebook only to delete it and "like" your status instead.

43. At your funeral, everyone will weep except for your son. He has never been one to cry for the dead. As a child he always thought something was wrong with him because of this. One day, while filling his daughter's inflatable swimming pool, the grief will spontaneously hit him like a wrecking ball wrapping itself around an ancient cathedral.

44. Life is longer than you could ever imagine. Eternity is shorter than you think.

45. Mrs. Hines was a failed novelist before turning to teaching to pay the bills. That thank you email you sent her was the only thing that convinced her she wasn't a complete failure at that.

46. Nobody blames you for S's death. She doesn't blame you either. There was nothing you could've done to save her from that sickness inside her heart that led her down a path nobody could follow.

47. That kid you chased down after seeing him scratch an 'X' in your

car was grateful you didn't tell his father. The old man beats him enough without having an excuse to do so.

48. The philosopher was right: we'll never step foot in the same river twice. The poet was only half right: what will survive of us is love, but so, too, will our hate.

49. S hated your spaghetti. The only reason she ate it is because you're the one who made it for her.

50. The hours you sat with your son after his wife's operation went terribly wrong meant more to him than all the cars and pairs of shoes and gaming systems you bought him ever could.

51. *Pixie* was picked up by a young couple not long after losing her way from home in a white fog of snow. She was loved every day of her life, spoiled by a little girl who couldn't fall asleep at night without first feeling her tiny frame pressed against her belly in the bed. She lived to be older than most dogs, but she never forgot that boy who would sneak her bites under the table as a puppy.

ON THE BENEFITS OF
A LEGO HEART WHICH
UNLIKE HUMAN HEARTS
CAN BE REBUILT AGAIN
AND AGAIN KNOWING THE
RESILIENCE OF THEIR
DELICATE CONSTRUCTION
EVEN AS THEY'RE BEING
SMASHED AGAINST
SOMETHING LIKE A HOUSE
OR TREE TRUNK OR EVEN
YOUR DADDY'S OLD PICKUP
TRUCK WITH THE MISSING
LEFT REARVIEW MIRROR
AND FAULTY CAB LIGHTS

In my mind, I had already built a Lego wall around the perimeter
of the yard, tall as the Siamese twin magnolia trees I sometimes sat
in perched on a beam nailed between two gnarled branches keeping
watch armed with a sawed-off Nerf gun loaded with all the ugliest
marbles from my collection and stealing bites from a camouflage
thermos full of lime Jell-O, daddy's second favorite flavor next
to orange. Though it wasn't the most effective deterrent against
trespassers - spraying out a wide wobbly arc of plastic rain made
forceful more by gravity than the simple spring-loaded mechanism
of the gun itself - it didn't take long for kids to learn just because
he was spending the week in a special hospital I wasn't about to let

his law go unpunished. Every time I would tag the back of a head or graze a bare hand or bullseye the small of a back, his reminder that I was man of the house now would ripple through me. If kids were dumb enough to crash through their screen door complaining to their parents, it would be them who got in trouble, not me. They had been warned not to come around. Back then the imposing figure of daddy standing in the yard like a sentient scarecrow, with his leathery Texas skin and calloused hands made for sawing and combination side-squint permascowl let all the neighborhood know it was a sin to cut through his yard, which served as a shortcut to the middle school, stadium, and Murphy Park – a dark-stained configuration of elaborate wooden castles with sharp edges perfect for picking up splinters and a jumbo concrete formation for water treatment we called The Heap, which all the young kids would climb upon and leap off of breaking their falls with their fingers, and teenagers would visit at night to do all the things that teenagers do at night. Only a little black girl my age who must've been new in town was dumb enough to escort her baby brother - who always wore the same pair of overalls and dangled the same string of snot from the same right nostril which came to rest against his lip - to the park every day through the private property of my newly inherited lawn. I first welcomed her to the neighborhood with a flurry of blue marbles, which she must've mistaken for a game, laughing as she zigged then zagged to safety. Day two she counter-acted, spotting me through a break in the branches, whipping up a pinecone. Day three, she shouted up something about whether my daddy was really crazy or not and I shot her between the eyes. That afternoon I heard the news: that this time daddy had shaved his arm too deep, so while my family sat inside studying their shoes pretending to enjoy a pity feast, I sat on the porch building a massive Lego heart just to piece it apart, brick by brick, click by click. When that bored me, I took to smashing it against the side of the house, flinging it at tree trunks, shattering it against daddy's old pickup truck with the missing left rearview mirror and faulty cab lights. The next day I abandoned my post, gluing the pieces together and dropping it from the top of The Heap. The girl, who must've been behind me for some time, told me she heard about my daddy. Down below, the heart hadn't survived the fall, but before I could loose all the sad stabbing my eyes felt a pair of lips on my lips, something like liquid stars swimming inside my stomach. And so we sat in a wooden Camelot holding hands to avoid the contraction of splinters together. Years later, someone would tell me Jell-O is made from the boiled bones of animals and this would come as no big surprise. Everything would make sense up to that point: the way anything good could only ever be bought with equal but opposite suffering.

POSTLUDE TWO

There is the story of the girl with a cactus heart who, upon waking every morning would find in the bathtub a key to a different door. The story of the girl who would, upon scooping sleep from her eyes and pouring a water spout down her throat to sate the prickling inside her chest, stumble to the bathroom, yank back a quartz curtain and claim her key before venturing out into a large, many storied clockwork dollhouse to discover which door her day would contain. The story of the doors, which would come in all shapes and sizes, colors and textures: some weathered and scuffed as if by claw, some teak, some tinfoil, some oblong, some furry, some glazed like salted meat. The story of the unlocking—the twist of a wrist, the music produced from a rococo mechanical click. The story of the day she renounced the key to carve a door of her own in the chandelier. The story of the day she forewent dowsing to let her cactus heart harden to a rock-candied shell, before eating it.

RULES TO WIN THE GAME

"It's a hard world for little things"

—The Night of the Hunter

The Game began around the time we discovered monsters were real. Theo, our eldest brother, started it the day he came into the center of the living room and declared he was no longer Theo but The Noir. Of course, none of us had any idea what it meant but we would learn in the coming weeks that it involved him wearing a long musty trench coat two sizes too big (it smelled like a bingo parlor), and a crushed hat with a feather gliding out of the top that would catch the kitchen light and shiver silvery, like a fish leaping out of water tickled by the sun.

Then he would hang around in corners all afternoon, smoking rolled paper while talking in a strange grown-up language none of us could translate. "You're barkin' up the wrong tree, toots," or, "Sorry dollface, but I don't know who that is," he would say, shrugging, puffing imaginary fumes whenever little Emilia would address him by the name of his old identity. The more I think about it, the more I suspect Theo might have known about the existence of monsters long before any of us.

The rules were never formally discussed but in time we all had an implicit understanding of The Game.

RULE: Everything is The Game.

Everyone is a player, whether they know it or not.

Emilia got her first fifty points when she died and was reborn The Zombie. She began shambling, lagging one foot and slurring her speech. She would sit on the sofa eating a bowl of brains in the morning, her shredded pink bunny Pogo Rex tucked tight between her kneecaps hemorrhaging clumps of cotton, his head dangling by a string.

Not long after that, Big Little Ray got his first points by donning a green hoodie with half-cut paper plates duct taped to the back and colored to look like scaly bumps. He announced he was The Crocodile, warned us to avoid the floor or risk having our feet snacked on or - god forbid - our bodies devoured entirely. He would slither around, dragging his enormous belly across the carpet, snapping at toes that weren't high enough off the ground, a makeshift snout wrapped around his jaw with jagteeth and two gaping cardboard cutout nostrils. Theo would ring a bell and that would be our cue to seek higher ground. Sure, we all hated having to elevate ourselves, pinned on tiny islands of furniture, but that was his rule and there was no way around it. Later, we would learn the trick of tossing down potato chips, which allowed us to shuffle by while Ray was busy chomping on the bait. We would all use that one to get around the house.

Ben eventually caved in, too - he was the oldest next to Theo. He knotted up his greasy hair with chopsticks, strapped a broken broom on his back and began bowing to everyone and meditating on the linoleum counter top all day. He called himself The Samurai. Emilia didn't know what that meant, but it made her laugh to see him battling the Crocodile through the swampish corridors of the house, yapping gibberish and waving his splintered sword like a kung fu cartoon. I think he was secretly Emilia's favorite. When he would give her a paper lotus she would blush three shades of pink, slur "Fankkk yeewwww."

*****

Everyone had their points except for me until the Sunday Theo slid up beside me and ignited a conversation. "Gotta light?" he asked, a toothpick stabbed between his teeth. After handing him some invisible matches, he rattled the box that wasn't there and shot me a suspicious look. "Say, what's your name lil fella?" Of course I couldn't think of anything flashy. "What you have is the look of a gunfighter—The Wild West." He was trying his best to help me out, you see, to get me into The Game. "Tough guy eh? Thanks for the tinder, kid. Twenty points for your troubles!" he said, and then winking, "I got my eye on you, mack." Then he leapt over The Crocodile, who was napping on a mattress in the middle of the floor, drizzling croc-slobber on The Zombie's leg. (She could get away with sleeping so close because she was already dead and her rotting skin was unsavory to The Crocodile's reptilian palate.)

  The Noir was still sharply eyeing me from a corner when we both heard the front door creak and the sinister jangling of keys, and we knew the Emperor of Black Rainbows was home for the day.

RULE: The Game is secret. The Emperor is never to know
of its existence.

Part-dragon, part-vampire, part-troll, The Emperor was the most evil monster in our tiny kingdom, and wore the face of a man as a clever disguise. He was always choosing a subject and taking them back to the Lair - what we called the peeling tin shed in our backyard with the hissing black light bulb - doing all kinds of mad scientist stuff in there. He'd come in and gather us up and choose one, just one, for the night. Then we'd watch him lead away our unlucky sibling with his mustard yellow finger-nailed hand.

It was a sinister kind of lottery. We all knew what would happen next, because we had all "won" at some time or another. He'd give you the Black Rainbow Punch - a syrupy medicine in an amber jar that always stayed full - and you'd be out cold, and when you woke up the next morning you'd be missing something: chunk of heart, lump of lung, half a stomach, quarter brain lobe. You never really knew what and that's what made it so scary. You might feel your heart ticking and never suspect it was gone forever, swimming in some coffee can on a wobbly shelf in the Lair. You could feel something, though. It hurt in the strangest places - embarrassing places - and you knew it was pain but only the slightest trace of it. The Punch would convince you it was all in your head. You'd believe it, because it was better that way.

The Noir would tell us to go ahead and drink the Punch because it was only when you woke up during one of The Emperor's organ-fests that you might see your lung in his hands and die on the spot. What you don't know will keep you alive, The Noir said.

These days though, he hardly ever took The Samurai or

The Noir anymore; I figured it was because The Samurai had his broom-sword and The Noir, well, he was The Noir. Me, The Zombie, and The Crocodile were his favorite test subjects now, The Zombie especially, who, aside from munching on human flesh all the livelong day, was a kind and trusting soul, clueless and completely oblivious to The Emperor's evil ways.

*****

On this day, we could tell The Emperor was feeling not-too-hot because he immediately reached for his Deathproof Tonic from the cabinet: a careful concoction of crushed bone, the ground up bits of our collective missing organs (minus the hearts - these he liked to keep as souvenirs), 12 % lava, 20% dog pee, and all of it spiked with the tears of our deceased Empress, who had been a much kinder ruler to us all before dying of a Voodoo curse.

Some say after The Empress passed, that's when The Emperor went mad and began the slow transformation to diabolical super fiend, but myths abound. Hard to tell what the truth is or isn't sometimes. The way it happened is never the same thing as the true story, The Noir tried to explain to me once. When I asked him about the Empress he told me she had been known for her red hair, but that her spirit was locked away in the Lair now and that was that. He flicked his paper cigarette, told me never to ask about her again.

RULE: The Empress is history. Don't ask.

I suspect if it hadn't been for the Tonic, The Emperor might have been slain long ago, but with the unholy stuff swimming in his blood, he was invincible. "There has to be a way to defeat him," The Samurai often thought aloud. "No," Theo would silence him. "There is no way."

*****

The first thing The Emperor did after getting the Tonic in his system that night was stumble into the living room and lure The Zombie over to his lap. He was quick to coax her with the Punch. "Take your medicine, creepy," he told her, pouring a capful. As she downed it he poured another. We watched him bob her on one knee, his teeth all pearly and fake. Sitting on the carpet, we could make out the rows of cavities that he hid so well from everyone else, those big black rotting stumps invisible from every other angle.

After a moment he dug around in his pocket and came out with a red rubber ball. He handed it off to The Zombie, laughing his grating laugh, and she took the bait. Just like that. Easy as pie. They were heading out the door, and the skies were growing a bruised purplish. We watched her skip all the way into the Lair, where Black Rainbows grew and twisted out of the walls like razorblade roses.

"Wonder what he'll take tonight?" The Crocodile said, twirling his tail made out of a bunch of cut up and tied-together water hoses.

"Maybe a chunk of brain. Maybe a kneecap. Who the hell knows?" The Samurai said, sharpening his sword with a coat hanger. The Noir perched on the counter, folding an Ace of Spades in half, a dark glint in his eye.

"Whatever he wants. He won't ever stop. Unless—"

We watched the Noir form the shape of a pistol with his right hand and pull the trigger. We imagined it bursting through the glass, splintering tin and burrowing itself a cozy home deep in The Emperor's skull.

*****

That night in the fuzzy lime twilight of the living room, as we lay sprawled like mutts on the floor, I could hear The Emperor creeping back inside. The glass door opened and shut with barely a sliding hush, and his black boots grazed by my head as he deposited the sleeping Zombie on the corner of our yellowing mattress. You'd think a man as big as him would hammer the ground but his walk was a clean gutter cat prowl. No, it was the breathing that gave him away, always the breathing: the way he would suck in air like a too-narrow chimney choking on smoke before shooting it out with a crippled cough.

I heard the lock on his door. Then, somewhere in the room I heard The Crocodile fart, The Samurai shifting in his sleep to parry the phantom blast.

The eerie green light from the VCR fell upon The Noir, whose wide-awake eyes were locked on to the sputtering ceiling fan with its one blade missing. I watched him spread a ragged sheet over The Zombie's feet. He noticed me, too, and I pretended to sleep. He raised up a bit, back to the wall, put his hand inside his trench coat. (We all slept in our clothes because it was safer that way.) He came back out with that imaginary revolver. This time he polished it with a rag that wasn't there. Flicked it to one side. Dug in his front pocket and brought out nothing, but it was like he was rolling that nothing around in his hand like loose bullets. Pushed six in the chamber. Click. Spun it once. Whoosh. Clapped it shut. Snap. Then, he put it away, tucked it back inside that strange, oversized coat of his. Finally he curved his hat over his face and turned over to sleep.

That's when I knew The Noir was doing cartwheels on the edge of crazy.

That night I dreamed of The Empress. In it, her bones kept bending back in impossible positions. She was bald and ugly, her lips an unnatural shade of blue, all chapped and peeling and terrible. Her eyes were gone, hollowed like olives with the pimentos sucked out, and she kept calling to me from inside this giant birdcage. "Out. Out," she kept muttering. I couldn't stand how bad she looked. She had been so beautiful in pictures I had seen. Now, reduced to this. "Out. Out."

The next morning when I yanked my head from my pillow, I shook off the sweat but I couldn't shake the dream. Out. I kept hearing it ping around in my brain. Out. Somewhere in that shed, The Empress was being held against her will, I knew it. The Noir said it himself. I couldn't stand it. Don't you know it's a horrible thing to feel trapped and powerless. It's a horrible thing to feel small. I began to hatch a plan to get her out of there.

I knew the only way I would survive inside the Lair was with Deathproof Tonic to keep the Black Rainbows at bay, so the next morning I strategically positioned myself below the cabinet where the Tonic was stored after The Emperor had already left for the day. I waited until the Crocodile lurked for his breakfast. Soon enough, that bell rattled, and we all took to higher ground.

The Crocodile slithered by, and as everyone watched him sniff The Zombie's toes through her shredded socks, I opened the cabinet and tucked the Tonic in my waistband.

Now, I knew what I was doing was punishable by torture. If The Emperor ever suspected someone of messing with his magical artifacts, we'd all pay the consequence. So as I took the bottle, I noted how it was positioned: label facing out, just left of the cracked mug with "World's Greatest Daddy." I'd have to put it back exactly. No room for error, not with The Emperor.

When it was safe, everyone hopped down and went about their usual routine. That is to say: The Zombie hobbled over to the television, bumping along with poor Pogo Rex by his frayed ears. The Crocodile yawned and scuttled beneath a table, going belly up and blowing snot bubbles through his leathery green snout. The Samurai folded paper flowers in the center of the living room. As for the Noir, he sat facing the window looking out over the wild tangle that surrounded the Lair, where dead trees posed like petrified bouquets of snakes, and the long brown grass and tall haunted weeds buzzed with bad omens. We all imagined freakish things in there, giant half-cricket half-dogs mutated and spliced together by The Emperor just for fun.

I knew I couldn't think too long about those kinds of

things if I wanted to rescue The Empress. I locked myself in the bathroom and turned the faucet on full blast. Sat on the commode twisting the cap off of the funny square-shaped bottle, the stuff inside sloshing and glinting in the sickly-yellow light. I poured some in a Dixie cup and tried to pretend it was medicine. I clamped my nose and swallowed quick. All I could taste was the 20% dog pee, enough to make my eyes sting and water. Over and over I refilled it. I nearly threw it back up into the bathtub, but I counted back from thirteen until it passed.

Stumbling out into the hall I felt dizzy. The Noir was the only one I was really worried about getting past, and I might have scrapped the whole plan if he hadn't been so busy with his eyes glued to the television screen, watching movies The Empress would've never let us watch in a hundred years.

They all had titles like The Big Shot or The Big Sleep or The Big Kill—he was a sucker for anything with 'Big' in the title I guess. I didn't understand the movies but The Noir, he spoke their language. He memorized all the lines. His hero was some guy named Humphrey with a face rough enough to sharpen pencils.

As I inched by, The Noir perked up, his head turned but only slightly. I was busted, I was sure of it. But he didn't say anything then. Even when I could see myself in the TV, and I could see that he was watching my reflection in the screen crossing the room. It wasn't until I was tugging on the sliding glass handle that he spoke up. Without turning to face me, without even giving any clear indication that he was addressing me at all, he said "Don't be late." That's what he said. For what? I couldn't tell you, but I wasn't about to hang around to find out.

Outside, I watched the shed looking mean with its zigzag rows of stripped paint like rusty, rain-rotted teeth. The high weeds waved, hiding a hundred ugly somethings I hoped would stay hidden long enough for me to get by them. When rain started to slant down upon me, I could feel my shoes turning into cast iron frying pans.

I could just make out the top of The Noir's head in the window, that feather of his shining through the dirt-caked window pane. It seemed like some magical charm to me, reminding me there were still places in the world where Black Rainbows didn't grow. Where wild colors were still able to breathe brightly, untouchable and true. With that in mind, I counted backwards from thirteen and found myself at doom's doorstep with the black bulb hissing just over me, an army of vines ready to tangle me up as they sensed the Tonic, shrinking back. One thing I was figuring out about the Tonic: it seemed to make you alert and sleepy all at the same time.

The first thing I saw inside was the long table that The Emperor splayed his subjects out on, deep fingernail trails in the wood. Row after row of dark stained cabinets. On the wall there was a board with rows of hooks that held various torture devices, surgical tools for cutting flesh and pounding bone, all brand new-looking. Shiny. You could tell he took pride in them. All around the room, there were high shelves with assorted shoe boxes, paint buckets, empty jars, potato sacks, plant pots, half-cut milk cartons, and hollowed out sleepy-eye dolls with egg-shaped heads, some with nails sticking through their faces, jutting through their noses or twisting out of their cheekbones. I knew our hearts were up there somewhere. First, I would concentrate on finding The Empress though.

I crawled up on the table to get a better look, but I was still feeling the effects of the Tonic and it was becoming tougher to focus. It dawned on me that I could have been tricked, because what I was now feeling felt a lot like the Black Rainbow Punch, and if that was the case I knew I would soon slip away and be out all afternoon, maybe forever. The Emperor would find me there on the table passed out, and he wouldn't take just a piece then, he'd take the whole thing. He'd be greedy.

So, naturally, when I went wobbly and fell from the table, landing hard on my knee cap, I was sick with shame. I had tried to use The Emperor's own medicine against him, but I should have known he was too clever for that. Real monsters always are.

RULE: You can't cheat the Game, even when it cheats you.

I might have been bleeding but I couldn't tell. The only thing I could do was drag myself to the nearest cabinet, feel my way inside before blacking out. If I was going to be found there, I hoped I would stay asleep through it all.

When I came to, I found I was still holed up inside that cabinet. My bottom was numb, and I had a pretty bad headache pinching the right side of my brain. I poked my head out to take a look and saw that it was growing dark through a window, clouds like black balls of fur scuttling across the sky, dusk spreading slow over the thorny trees like a star-stained blanket. Then I could hear the mutant mutt-crickets chirping through the walls, grating their entrails like violin strings, declaring the Black Rainbow Hour begun. It was too late.

My first instinct was to spill out and head for the house, and I was about ready to elbow the flap and make a break for it when I heard the shed door break first. Then the hacking cough. I pulled the cabinet door closed.

In walked two bodies; the obvious presence, and another, softer one. I heard something like the thump of dead weight. Zippers zipping, buttons snapping. Hands rubbing together like sandpaper hard at work.

I tried to spy through the crack, trying so hard not to breathe. I had to wrap my arms around my mouth. All I could see was The Emperor towering over the table through a thin slit, caressing hair or - something. Sharpening blades or cleaning his surgical torture apparatus.

It was then that I saw it, high on a shelf above The Emperor's silver head of hair: a Voodoo doll with two 'X's for eyes, perfect stitch-mouth, red mangy mane of hair like a waterfall on fire. The moment I saw it I knew it had to be her. In my mind, I imagined being able to reach her and tuck her away in my pocket along with my brothers and sister, stealing us off to a bright city so deep with alleys, so crowded with people the Black Rainbows would never find us. We could be safe in a place like that, happily lost and never alone among a sea of strangers.

I guess I imagined too hard though, because in my dreamreaching, I lost my balance and spilled out of the cabinet in full view of The Emperor.

RULE: Stay safe inside your head.

He stopped what he was doing, waiting for me to stand up. I shouldn't have, but I did.

As if I had emerged through a long dark tunnel, braved the warm comfort of that darkness for so long only to smash into a blue wall of even more terrifying daylight, I saw everything upon the table. I had to fall right back down.

In the pit of my stomach I could feel it wasn't natural. The tiny body splayed on the table like that, like a living doll. The living doll spread out and open on the table like a clockwork plaything, and The Emperor with his hands upon it all, making use of it, turning those cogs, moving and contorting the mechanical parts for his own perverse amusement. My baby sister, fast asleep.

Fast asleep: the one thing I found peace in.

RULE: The way it happened is never the same thing
as the true story.

Black Rainbows flitted about the room now, and I felt myself losing it, the tears came in a continuous rush. My stomach collapsed and a great wave of shame and fright flowed through me, like burning and cold all at once.

"Dear boy," The Emperor addressed me, standing over me as I lay crumpled and sobbing at his ankles. He ran his forked tongue twice over his gums. "Dear, dear boy." Whistling, he meandered over to the corner, picked out a dull-looking hacksaw. He slung it aside, gripping a hammer before finally deciding on a simple screwdriver instead. "This'll work, doncha think?" He stood over me again, smiling, his cavities fully exposed. "C'mere boy. Let's see what makes you tick."

And I don't know where he came from, but suddenly The Noir was there with us, standing at the door, his hands in the front of his coat pocket, cursive wisps crawling up from the tip of his cigarette. "Say, buster, we've got some business to settle," he said, calling out The Emperor. "I'm here to collect."

The Emperor turned to face him. Through his knees I could see The Noir, who flung me a wink before spitting out his cigarette.

"One thousand points for helping me slay The Emperor, kid," The Noir said, and then he aimed his index finger point blank at The Emperor, who began to laugh. The room flashed white, and then all that was left was a miniature fog of smoke hanging in the air, The Emperor laid out beside me on the concrete with a hole the size of a grape in his forehead, gushing black blood.

*****

The next thing I remember is being back inside the house where The Crocodile was cheering, jubilantly proclaiming to all the kingdom, "The Emperor is dead! The Emperor is dead!"

Whatever power he had held over us had fallen away, I knew it, but still something was terribly wrong. The Noir stood at the sink, frantically emptying out the Deathproof Tonic that I had left in the bathtub, the Deathproof Tonic that The Emperor had not been able to find that afternoon, which had left him temporarily vulnerable. The Noir peeked through the chipped blinds, then spoke: "You did good, kid, but they'll come for you now. They'll come for you to try to get to her, but they'll never get her will they?" He slapped me on the back and tousled The Zombie's ketchup-locks. Then, he plucked the feather from his hat and put it in my hand, wrapping my fingers around it for me.

"Here's looking at you, kid," he said, holding the front door open for me and The Zombie to escape. The Samurai and The Crocodile watched on, with their eyes exchanging the terms of a silent pact that I knew would never be broken between us. I could hear the dreamy murmur of sirens in the distance, long red and blue shrieks wailing, howling the night into a shredded song of youth. I counted back from thirteen, grabbed The Zombie, and, for the first time in our lives, we were free.

"Hold my hand," I said as she began to bawl. "Don't look back." Then we were off, winding through birdbath lawns, navigating by panic. Only once did I stop to tie her shoe and stab the feather behind her ear, which seemed to calm her some.

I could feel my big frying pan feet begging me to turn around. To find a good place to hide. To sprout wings and sail the marbled sky. I was afraid because I understood everything at that moment. I knew all the things we weren't supposed to know. I could feel the hollow space inside where my heart had once been, ripping itself wider and wider. Then I could see where downtown started and the old neighborhood ended, where the gravelly pavement became slick and oily, and the swaying magnolias turned into stark, soulless streetlights, where the crowns of the trees became the wide rims of soot-belching smokestacks. There was a sick, empty feeling crawling up my throat, scabs everywhere, in the bushes the trees the sidewalks the skin of my hand trembling in my pocket. In short, Black Rainbows lurked around every corner, but then I remembered something my brother once said, the day before he died and became someone else.

If you can just make life into a game, you can make it up as you go, and they can't touch you. It won't matter whether you win or lose then, because even if you lose, you win.

I hesitated, just long enough to make out a bird - or was it a bat? - diving upward into a shimmerwhite pool of sky. On a rooftop, a storm-beaten weathervane slung itself around, its brass finger pointing west, toward the city steeped in neon blur, buzzing like an electric orchard.

Finally, I understood what The Game was for, and who. I watched moonlight chase its way along the razor's edge of the feather behind Emilia's ear: our very own Black Rainbow ward, keeping the colors true.

RULE: The only way to win The Game is to never stop playing it.

"One hundred points for not crying," I heard myself say to Emilia. As we zagged through an alley, leaving our old lives behind and making up new ones along the way, I knew I was a terrible liar. I hoped I would be as good at fighting monsters as the Noir had been. "And call me The Cowboy." The Enchanted City lay before us in the distance, floating in a mist of melancholy dream.

SUNKEN DREAMERS'
ALMANAC

Zero Percent Chance of Showers

In the half painted room L pushes pills into her pillowcase. Off
her meds since the baby shower postponed itself indefinitely she's
sick of not knowing the question when the answers are all around
her: there is cutlery in the counter, orange vials that vow sympathy
sleep, a loaded escape plan in the closet. As the sun slopes the lean
shadows slay, slow dance across an unfinished wall. Clock clicks
nervous teethchatter as L drowns a bassinet in the bathtub.

Tornado Warning

M settles down on his usual bar stool & orders a round of twisters,

on the verge of quitting a marriage marred by emotional flat

lines & a heart from Mars. Since the doctor delivered his news,

the stranger in his wife's skin has taken over, usurped her body

& pumped her brain full of acid. Ever since intimacy has been

foreign planet, her alien alphabet its mother-tongue. On his seventh

shot he thinks: the lonely gears that grind a man's heart cannot be

unwound. Around the bar there are several holes to fill the hole,

but tonight the gutters have teeth & there are devils everywhere.

Dust flickers through night's blue arc as M crawls into his truck,

drums the door with his fingers & accepts his handsome cage.

Twists the machine alive, too lost to know how lost he really is.

High Winds

H battles bikes off the turnpike. Coughs graffiti on bathroom stalls
in his off hours, stalls the hours getting off with his girlfriend J the
freshman. Gnarly since he was knee high, gnarls his knees sky high
in the drained pool thrashing flesh until threshed legs beg for bolts,
until the sky bolts black & blue. Making art of his scars he swirls
scab frescos. Full crash expressionist, dangerous as life without
a helmet. All year he is curb-splendor, collision-crafting, bone-
grafting: jilted juggernaut in jackknife leather jacket armor. Sputters
his propellers all afternoon ditching class, catching ass only to catch
hell from the old man who caught news of his routine absence
from teacher Q. Finally retires from the old man's roost, tired
of the tired lectures he swallows living under his roof. Blowing
through red lights his renegade rocket horse slips a shoe, leaving
alpha rider sidewalk-docked until careening comes a run amok
truck out of the blue.

Cold Snap

Q pops a quiz every pep rally Friday. Picks out a new tie for every cute tail he curtails in detention, his highs entailing emotional entrails & youth addiction. Hides his sickness in the secrets he secretes on his sheets, behind the artificial whiteness of his teeth, only flashing his fangs to a limited audience of prey. Seethes a ring of skull upon his bedroom mirror as snow plows the world outside, while internal pipes bleed steam & burst, too brittle for below zero onslaught. Where human warmth once wrought remedy, now fresh rot floats spreading infection flotsam in the form of unfit-for-society fantasies. On her knees, his newest derelict devotee raises her 'D' until the freeze thaws & withdraws its glacier gaze. Then, alone behind his desk he sits moonlighting memories through the icy haze, thinking: The big bad wolf wasn't born that way - it took years of parental malpractice to make imperfect, a father with a subarctic heart & taste for young lupine spine.

Light Drizzle

J motors through the halls traipsing trash flashing ass, a mouthful of
motley moths eyeful of kerosene cocktail. Uses her sex tomahawk
for teenage survival, having learned the rules of combat in the
basement of a bunker, her drunk uncle taught her at a young age
to engage. Now she can't stop feeding her awful appetite, often
hungry she wolfs lashing lambs with an eyelash to feel normal.
Earns an 'A' in poly sci for spreading thighs, saves her shy cries for
under the bleachers listening to the pep rally ripple, rattling loose
metal while she loses her mental mettle. A secret bump in her belly
nobody knows boulders heavy on her shoulders, scolders her future
flammable to the touch of hope. In the natatorium she salutes the
floor with cherry vomit, green lights a gasoline kiss guzzling pool
cleaner. While the school anthem flaunts her own freakdom, she
flirts with a diving board, waltzing the watery edge. Blacking out,
counts her lucky scars & skitters through scabrous blue.

Flash Flood

The unborn jostles inside mama's belly. Not so much as a name
yet, the two outside voices have taken to calling her B for Baby, or
Blessing, or Burden, or Broken Birth Control. Voice X is small &
soft: sings sparks when all is calm, lacing the lonely catacomb air
with lullaby. Very large & scary is voice Y: wraps itself around the
silence like a full body zipper. Snags like a telephone wire noose
& then yanks up, greeting X's shrieks with a cold clack of bone
against wet bone, an occasional wash of siren. Everything is never
too late until it is. Everything is just a warning until it isn't. B is for
Beware. B is for Belly Filling Up With Blood. B is for Bodies, as
in, two found, one within the other, at the bottom of a pool. B is
for Bruises That Will Never Heal. B is for Bad Luck, That Poor
Mother, That Poor Child. B is for Blood That Never Deserved
To Bleed Out. B is for Bells, as in, church. B is for Black, as in,
the color that everyone wore. B is for Born, as in, never. B is for
Blanked Out, as in, as if nothing ever happened.

Hope as Furious Negation of Doppler Effect, or the Myth of Meteorological Predestination

That weather vanes lie. That every forecast is fickle: the imperfect meteorologist as slave to the uncertainties of weather, not the other way around. That though man has inherited the laws of the wild, the wild does not adhere to the laws of man. That just as clouds float where they want to float storms gather & break when they're ready to break, hearts divide & collide at their own terminal velocity not subject to the flimsy radars & barometers of fate. That all grace is tentative, constantly ending & unending together. That everything that sinks will rise again, in second skin. That tomorrow a blanket of fog that had obscured the torch-tips of tinny stars above could lift like accidental Baptism to lantern your way home.

POSTLUDE THREE

There is the story of the boy with an appetite for mirrors. The story of the many ways in which he would cook his mirrors for consumption: basted, kabob'ed, crème brulee'd, fricasseed. The story of the extinction of mirrors, having all been eaten by a glutton grown more handsome with each banquet of shards. The story of polished cutlery gone missing in the night, toasters, bumpers, hubcaps, sheets of ice, anything with a reflection. The story of clouds as condiment. The story of the boy who eventually ate the ocean, who could not be contained, who could not contain the Atlantic. The story of a stomach ache dilated to delirium, like scarabs on an origami Mars, or licorice fish tickling through the nipples of apocalypse.

PASSENGERS

This is the way the world ends
This is the way the world ends
This is the way the world ends
Not with a bang but with a whimper.

—The Hollow Men, T. S. Eliot

We left campus early Wednesday headed toward Texas because civilization was crumbling and everyone in the world was in denial except us. Naresh, who never talked, was driving (it was his car) and besides being a passive-aggressive closet gay, he was probably the most in-control out of all of us. Pike in the passenger seat, who talked all the time, had jelly beans in his lap, counting colors. He worked at a pharmacy so I guess counting them was a natural way for him to keep his mind busy. He couldn't stay still very long. It was a thing with him. Pike was a sex addict.

I prefer the backseat. I can do my poetry in peace.

An Original Comedy
by Oliver Sax

Two manikins tied to the train tracks
One manikin looks at the other and says
something

Along comes the train and slices their
heads offs

The road is conducive to the poet because, on the road, location is a constant illusion. Because everything is made of blinks, you never know if life is moving backwards, forwards, down, up, or all directional possibilities simultaneously. Even time forgets you if you go far enough (like that painting with the drippy clocks) and with nothing left to do, you watch. That's where the poetry comes from. The truth is, you're moving everywhere and nowhere together. The road is the only honest place.

Whenever it would get too quiet, Pike would begin. "Look, I'm not saying they're lesser or under us in any way, just that—chemically-speaking—women are more psychotic than men. Not something they can help, just the way things are…rotten luck of the cosmic draw. I don't blame them. They can't help they're nuts any more than we can help needing them so hard. Sometimes, you have to face the truth."

Pike had a name for all the women in his life. Eva Zoland was EZ Rider; Jodie Busby was The Incredible Spreadable Leg; Lisa White-Richardson, The Moaning Lisa; and then there was The Whore—that's what he called his mother. He hadn't seen the Whore since he was nine, when she remarried someone that wasn't his father—a dentist or some dopey profession like that. In truth, his real father was just as bad. But you don't call grown men 'whores,' you just call them men.

I had my own names for the pills. The round milky tablet with the + sign, I called Holy Spirit. It was like eating radiation—a mouthful of bees buzzing at a hundred times per second. Your teeth rattle and your tongue tingles all the way down your throat. Then you feel it fizzing in your bloodstream, pushing through veins and creeping into muscles like little neon streams of viscous starlight. The ends of your fingers shoot electricity and your knees become gushing volcanoes. The best part is, while the body's busy with all that, your mind empties and there's nothing left to think about. You're free, like a rock or a branch or a germ.

The bubblegum-pink capsule was called Angel of Truth; the blue pill, Revelator. The former liked to play with your metaphysical sensibilities; you could get very Einstein about very common things very quick. You might even see things as connected or meaningful. The latter did nothing for me.

A man at a gas station told us there was a huge drought going on in San Antonio, so for the rest of the time we were busy arguing a hypothetical: was it better to find a glass of water in the desert or the mirage of a glass of water? Because a glass of water would only really prolong things, stretch the whole torturous journey out but a mirage would be more honest therefore more compassionate. In the end, we all agreed it was better to find a glass of gin. Through Waco I was busy watching the glacier blue sky, the same color of the veins popping out along my arms like wires or tiny rivulets. Through Austin, we touched hot matches to our skin and lolled our heads out the window like shameless dogs. At one point, I saw a hot air balloon and it was such a pretty thing I wanted to shoot it down with a bazooka. Pike was trying to guillotine me with the window controls when the car jolted off to the side of the road and suddenly it was the Fourth of July where a patriotic booth was selling disposable thrills and destruction. Pike said he was feeling patriotic too. He wanted some black cats.

I found myself over at a table where a dusty man in a straw

chair sipped ice tea from a molasses glass. A collection of assorted kaleidoscopic bottles and jars lined his table—beautiful empty bottles that glittered in the sun.

Nearby, soda-bottle chimes strung from a tree limb clanked impetuously as little girls danced beneath sprinkler rain in their ragged summer dresses. They licked at the air, catching it on their tongues and looking stupid but beautiful. A boy with a pirate patch picked off cars with his cap revolver. For a minute, I wanted to gather them all up and kidnap them and take them away to a place where they could dance under the sprinklers forever but Pike was back in the car and calling me.

An Original Comedy
by Oliver Sax

Two manikins walk in to a marriage counselor

Question comes crashing along:
Problem?

One manikin sniffs and speaks up

'Our paper
mache relation
ship's sailing'

Soon after,
they catch the train

Back in the car, I tried to remember what it was like to be young. It's not easy being a kid when you're smarter than all of your teachers and you're just now learning your place in a people with a legacy of enslavement, rape, extortion, etcetera etcetera, ad infinitum. And then one day you get kicked out of school for plagiarizing your paper because the assignment was a waste of your time and everyone's time really, even though it wasn't really about plagiarism at all so much as calling Mr. Bell, your incompetent stuttering history teacher, a 'fuckshit' for referring to the Native Americans as 'Indians' even though they never touched India or heard of Jabalpur, Gandhinager or Vishakhapatnam.

You got to be an Againster to get by in this world. You know who said that? Bogart: the goddamn wiseman.

I got to thinking about a whole lotta things that didn't make any sense. Like how there could be a rebellion in Heaven if Heaven is supposed to be Paradise. Or the Nobel Prize being founded by the same guy who invented dynamite, a conception perfectly realized in World War II by its effectiveness in blowing the limbs off soldiers. Or a world that could assassinate Gandhi. The list just got longer as stars were popping out and the last thing I remember before falling asleep was the car off to the side of the road and all of us trying to sleep, except Pike who was masturbating in the backseat. The moon shooting through the window illuminated a helpless desperation in his eyes and I realized he wasn't enjoying it. Naresh, somehow, was sleeping like a baby. I had seen the same look in his eyes before but in other contexts. When he would talk to his father on the phone, he would get really sad because apparently he was some kind of Indian royalty and though he had lived in America since he was three, his parents still believed in arranged marriage. They also chose not to believe in homosexuality, like it was a myth or the goddamn Greenhouse Effect. His parents had recently found him a fetching bride, an exotic beauty named Bezilda or something. "I'm not into Indian girls," he once told me. If he couldn't tell his own friends the truth about liking dicks, how could he ever tell his parents? Between Pike and Naresh, I couldn't decide which had been dealt the crummier hand. When it came down to it, it didn't make any difference anyways because no matter how good a hand you get, what's wrong is the game. Before I made myself shut my eyes, I remember seeing a dramatic eerie cross lit up like a fast-food joint sign. Underneath could be read SALVATION except the ION was burned out, leaving only SALVAT cutting through the night with its holy jumbo buzz.

* * *

Next we were in a greasy diner in Victory, Texas waiting for Dorothy the waitress to bring us silverware even though we all ordered chicken strips with gravy and steak fries. B-B-B-Benny and the Jetssssssssss was playing in the background and I thought it was funny that my preconception of Texas involved saloon music playing in every establishment, like it was a law or something. Dorothy dropped the silverware off and Naresh sneezed because she smelled like apple pie and hairspray. Pike watched her thighs bounce like buoys. There was a stuffed yak head on the wall looking inquisitive. War was on the TV but it was only a rerun.

I was busy making a list of the top ten misunderstood people.

Houdini

Joan of Arc

The Big Bad Wolf

Bartleby

J.D. Salinger

Caligula

Captain Hook

Nietzsche

Leopold Bloom

Wile E. Coyote

When Pike disappeared with some cowgirl with big shoulders, I walked back out to the car because that's where the jelly beans were. I unzipped the baggy and put it back. Someone had left his revolver in the glove compartment. It's ok though because it was Texas. Soon I was tripping on three colors and, letting the passenger seat glide back, I watched clouds like tumbleweeds moving faster than I'd ever seen clouds move before.

Naresh was back in the car buttering a biscuit in the front seat when I woke up. Where did he get that biscuit? I thought. Then I realized we were still parked at the diner.

"Pike is with Marlena," Naresh informed me.

"Hey, can I have some of your biscuit?" I said. He handed me half and the butter knife too. I gobbled it up and put the knife in the glove compartment because it still had butter on it.

An hour later, Pike came screeching out jangling his keys. His dick was half out of his pants. Behind him a mob of cowboys were stampeding. It was a funny sight until we remembered he was with us. A mustached fellow with a white vest and the biggest hat (he must have been the leader) was banging on my window as Pike twisted the ignition and we were jostling through a parking lot. When we were on the road, Pike began, "Sometimes, you have to break some hearts."

We drove until we were sure the Texas Rangers weren't still after us and we were lost in a suburban neighborhood. We were walking around in an undeveloped house and Pike was peeing on a hammer in the corner.

A dog wandered in through the door and I thought it was rabid even though it had a leash. I don't know why I thought it was. Maybe because it looked too happy. It had sand in its hair and the tail looked broken. Good doggy, I said. I only said it because I was afraid, though. If it got any closer I would have punted it. Good doggy.

"My dad has a dog just like this one. He loves that goddamn dog," Naresh said.

Since Naresh was warming to the pup, I decided to move outside. I walked around heaps of trash and wood and nails and buckets of sludge and bricks and puddles of putty and all the bullshit that goes into the building of a house, until I noticed a rock with a flower growing out of it. At first I didn't think it was real. When I carried it back inside, Naresh was taping up the dog with red paper or something and he looked really busy so I decided to ask Pike about it, who was upstairs busting bottles.

I told him I found it and it was real but he kept saying that flowers couldn't grow out of a rock because it was a scientific impossibility. Soon, he convinced me that the rock-flower I was holding wasn't possible and could never be possible so I tossed it out the window and decided to break a few bottles. About that time, we heard a series of pops and crackling and howling downstairs.

I thought it was World War III but when we went downstairs, Naresh was hovering over the pup, who looked fried in parts and bloody and hairless and terrible. Naresh had tears in his eyes and a look like he didn't know what happened…even though he was still holding a lighter in his hand and the rest of the black cats were in his other hand.

"It wasn't his fault. It wasn't his fault," he kept saying. Just kept repeating it over and over. He was waving his hand over the dog like he wanted nothing more than to touch it; to comfort it and apologize for the way the world was—the way it didn't explain anything. Pike looked like he was ready to throw up. He slipped outside.

Poor thing. The death of a dog has to be the saddest thing in the entire world. Little dog tears in black marble eyes. Because even when their chest is pumping hard and paws are scraping at the air and you can tell they're in fight-for-life agony…they still have that dopey smile on their face. Like they're still happy as ever just being a dog. Their mouths were designed that way. I was thinking it was the biggest indignity.

A moment later, Pike was back inside and aiming a revolver down through the dog's ear and then pulling the trigger and then standing over us all like a father figure.

"Sometimes, you have to shoot a dog," he said.

When we decided we couldn't just leave it there, we carried it out to the trunk and an old lady waved at us. We all waved back.

* * *

I woke up as the car was shaking off to the side of the road. Pike was yelling at me and grappling with Naresh and I thought maybe Pike was still angry at him about the whole dog incident. When I looked though, Naresh had a butter-knife to his throat and he was sawing away. I composed a poem, but this time only in my head.

An Original Comedy
by Oliver Sax

Three manikins at the edge of the world
One's losing his head

We managed to wrestle the knife away from Naresh and get him out of the car and hold him down until he was through weeping like a goddamn sheep on fire.

We stayed there like that for a long time. Just waiting for something to happen. For the world to pass. For everything to die or get old or transform into something else. When nothing happened though, we just sat down in the dirt. Pike went to the trunk and brought back the dog. We decided to hold a small funeral in the afternoon. We each said a few words. I wanted to recite a poem, something beautiful. The best I could do though was say a little something I could remember from a church I once visited. There was a black preacher there, a Miles Davis looking fellow I called 'Amen Brother' because that's what he said at the end of everything. I said what he said.

I was wishing I had kept that rock with the flower to bury with the dog. The strange things people do when they're in pain, I thought. Naresh was looking extra sad and I wanted to offer him a jellybean, but there were only seven left and I needed about that many for the long ride home.

Sometimes you have to shoot a dog, Pike said. I wondered how many dogs there were in the world. Maybe a billion. I wondered if that could ever be enough.

After the funeral, we walked until we found an abandoned shed. We lit it on fire and watched every board burning black within a rage of orange smoky curls. The Native Americans believed that the smoke rising up from their pipes would carry the breath of God down through the plume into their open mouths.

Part of me wanted to bury the bag beneath my feet, the same part of me that wanted to believe something better could bloom. It seemed like a moment in a movie where everything could turn around for the best. But this wasn't a movie. We weren't players on the stage of life and Shakespeare's an asshole for saying that. Whatever we were was really real and whatever was wrong was really wrong, and no matter how far we drove or how many dogs we exploded or pills I planted, things wouldn't get better because symbolism only works in stories.

And if life is a stage then I forgot my lines the day I was born, the audience is facing backwards, the director's backstage building a birdhouse, the writer is a shitty dramatist, and the theater's on fire.

Pike said something about us losing our minds. Naresh watched demons in the dirt. As the chemicals kicked in, I was the inner life of a balloon rising oblique through shredded cotton cloud.

RELIQUARY FOR THE TRAMPLED UNDERFOOT

I. *ballad of a bumble bee trapped in honey*

       That dizzying last summer we explored the one
billion possibilities of bumblebee assassination. We learned lacing
the curb with Dr. Pepper to lure them under a false pretense of
sweetness was easiest, most merciful, for the shadows of our black
devil shoe soles were guillotine-swift and double-quick to evict
the poor souls from their black and yellow striped cages. What the
hell is beeswax anyways? we wondered, watching the furry beasts
writhe in Wite-out on paper plates, or rattle in plastic Tupperware
tombs. We put them in ice trays in the freezer and waited, called it
a science experiment, while Count Chocula plinked into your cereal
bowl and the milk sloshed everywhere and you ate it with a fork.
You were just that kind of girl. Then you squeezed half a bottle
of honey into the empty bowl and funneled a baby bee through a
rolled up magazine, and for the first time in my life I felt guilty for
our senseless sin. Don't bees smell fear? I said, and you shook your
head. If they smell fear, surely they suffer fear themselves. I asked
you to stop and you told me it was no use, it was too late. As I
struggled to rescue our tiny prisoner from his undeserved fate with
a pair of tweezers, I didn't see you approaching with the hammer.
All I saw were the gooey guts on the blunt edge embedded in
amber ooze, the broken bowl wobbling across the tiles, your

vile curvature of lips and teeth. Let's go to your house, you said,

mentioning how your father would soon be home, and though

I agreed I was secretly angry with you. So as we sagged our way

there, dragging our bag of bones through the apricot dusk with

its inferno flash sweating sugar-heat, I took flight through the tall

grass, left you at the halfway mark on the hill. I thought I saw your

sticky fingers waving goodbye the night you went home and never

came back. Forgive me: I was too young to smell your fear.

II. *ballad of a wingless butterfly, torn asunder by unforeseen windstorm*

His habit comes naturally, an almost instinctual love of womblike warmth, hideaway places and secret graffiti. Folds his bones for hours on end, prostrates himself beneath the rumbling highway overpass under shotgun tailpipes, brake snarls, hiccupping honks and rattling metal. Something about being lost, tunnels and the cloak of crevices. There, he knows those hunting headlights will never find him. To be lost is to be found. He likes to ride the top of the enormous magnolia tree in the front yard during impromptu storms just to see if lightning will deign to strike. All it takes is once. He is unafraid to die. Nine years old. The bough sways his lithe bones, slams the cage of his body to and fro, but not enough to lift him up. Rain feels good to an open cut: Jesus' own antiseptic. There on the mottled bark, hunched inside a hole he spots the butterfly, paper wings hanging loose, daring to be ripped free. He is quick and merciful. When mother calls he ignores, the way she ignores Him. When He calls, he knows it's time to come down. Greeted at the peeling screen door by His crooked cowboy grin, dark leather skin and Old Testament handshake. The Old Man likes to crunch ice to a pulp when He goes to work on him at night. To be lost is to be found, he tries to remember, straightening his back and taking it. Afterwards, as he is made to recite selected passages from the Good Book, he makes sure to drip upon and smear those slick gold pages.

POSTLUDE FOUR

There is the story of the birdhouse having grown wings of its own, having flown far far away, tired of its insides serving as a cage for calculated wingbeats. The story of the inverted bird that ate the birdhouse whole, that flew impromptu into the moon mistaking it for a translucent lake of cheese. The story of a cubist rainbow where departed birdhouses are born again as the pink sorrow of scarecrows.

ESCAPOLOGY

*roll a d20

1-2

*in your mouth the stubborn stir of birds, their battered wingbeat birthing dust.
your clipped tongue in straightjacket embrace. his tall blue kiss in a dark room
suckling wasps through cellophane straws / lose half a childhood.*

3-4

*sneeze not & the closet will cloak you. sneeze & the closet will spit you out like
rotten teeth, like wet rat tails. your fleeting faith in cartoon logic: so long as you
don't look down the floor won't fall out from under you / roll again.*

5-6

*in the land of broken shoe lace tin can hills the orphan collectors ascend to
hunt, thirsty with cigarette eyes. haunt anything with residual color, suck pale
breath to gray the secret world. soil your sheets & keep this fingernail tally on
your stomach lining / lose the remaining half of a childhood.*

7-8

*careen your bunk bed into the clouds, sail safe & sound for now. sanctuary of
a child's game & imagination's arrow / move forward.*

9-10

*your mother in the nuthouse, her wrists raw from plastic cutlery. her growing
shriek a bag of bolts slow-emptying into a blender. the kingdom of her once*

sharp lullaby overgrown with thorned poppies & tangleweed. how she uses a
brick to slaughter all those moths regressed from butterflies in the night war.
but for one split second her frail mind solidifies, snaps back into focus, her love
pierces thru the infected walls: "none of this was your fault...none of this will
ever be your fault" / level up.

11-12

teenage runaway! better off on the streets than in the orphan factory (a) the
subtle art of disappearing, fading forward, sliding out of the scene into fake
Hollywood backdrops. (b) the not-so-subtle art of fucking fire with gasoline
genitalia. (c) strict diet of addiction, alcohol or your mother's pills. (d) minor
sublimation to taunt the wounds, petty crime skateboarding & graffiti / choose
one coping mechanism.

13-14

your father's funeral. a scab in your mind making mud of memory. too soon to
pick off so remain stuck in the muck of adolescence / lose a turn.

15-16

college. pyramids crumble & black clouds overhead. the sidewalks slash your
bare feet. even though the dragon is dead his ghost still haunts the skies. any
sunlight that touches you is scarring. sell your bed that still smells of his scales
& sleep on the floor / move back.

17-18

gaze in the mirror & gasp at the stranger with your stolen eyes - sunken
like the years - & every inch ravaged by the atomic bombs of youth. tired of
suffering the fallout, consider forfeiting / game over or continue?

19-20

all your life you've built up this fortress. all your life this fortress has never been strong enough. someday when you least expect it you come to find your hate has gagged on all its pretty shiny hopes of escaping reality, & what is left is what was there all along, crushed quietly underneath the thick shell of ruckus & rot, tucked beneath the glinting knives of memory longing to be sterilized: forgiveness for the obsolete beast. you look down at your daughter underfoot flapping her arms with the quickening hope of hummingbird wings & know she will be clean, she will be pure / with the game already won, drop the dice, look down, find a floor there to catch you.

ANTI-MIDNIGHT IN THE KINGDOM OF YES

Begin with a simple ward like a prayer so beautiful it cannot be spoken aloud, or a corpse so small one could not heap enough dirt to ply her light. Sometimes you would pretend to be the weather station & treat me to a forecast, like *expect a mudslide tonight in Toledo, tomorrow there will be snow in Tokyo.* We swallowed ourselves in the homecoming parade when we knew home was lost, buried our grace in the sidewalks so only the footfalls might find us. Television sang us to sleep those nights our tongues failed to fetch us our words. Patio chimes tapped out our shame, the dogs yelped our fence had been left open. & your silent face is Mandela music. I've never seen anything as sinless as your pale thin wrists - file under Things I Should Have Told You When I Had You Here in the Passenger Seat. There is a cathedral on the far side of town we could spy its steeple from our house. Tomorrow while the children let out from school they'll tear it down. But how the trees graft themselves to the lake, how the clouds hang from the moon like your memory swings from my chandelier: Remember this landscape, if nothing else, the way I still wrap my stain glass around your sunlight. This is where the ward ends, this is where you say goodnight, this is where you lean in close, pour your poison through my ears, whisper: *Of the hundred billion types of light you were my favorite.*

CONSEQUENCE OF SPLITTING THE ATOM

Progress is made in such ways as Sure & Cut Here & Bomb the Temples. We fed growth hormones to the angels for weeks then fed them glass to study the angles at which they fell from the sky. Froze the stars with radon gas to charge a surtax on light. In the barracks where we scientists slept the Great Radio would instruct us further. Under our pillows our protractors & holy polarimeters. Some terrorists rigged the particle collider to blow we relocated to the countryside, paid the farmers in data & slaughtered the sacred cows. Harpoons of spirit concentrate let loose in vaporous spurts, we siphoned the savage matter, refined it & pasteurized into a chemical cocktail, pumped it in through pneumatic tubes & increased our oral anatomies by 200%: elocutionary state of the art. That winter our tongues turned black, satellites began to topple from space. Beached on earth their frazzled husks hemorrhaged sparks. Helium rockets barely braved flight, skimming sky before lost in the atmosphere. All fuses refused. We returned to the sacred cows but the supply had been mercy-scalped, the ancients absconding to the west. Back in the barracks we found the tables had been lined with scalpels, the Great Radio told us the answer was inside us all along. *Go ahead*, it decreed, *make your contribution - just leave your blood tithe at the door.*

POSTLUDE FIVE

There is the story of the staircase found under the baby's tongue. The story of the tiny people who opt instead for the elevator in his left eardrum. The story of tsunamis caused by a tantrum over a stolen pacifier. The story of gravity broken in half by the popping of a purple balloon. The story of a mudslide crumpling teepees along follicles in the event of an exploded diaper. The story of a drought during belly button season.

COSMONAUTS / NOTS / KNOTS

Tonight H is building tiny antennas for a baby spacesuit. Never
seen antennas on a spacesuit before, I tease her. Sprawled on
the kitchen floor she smiles, bending back a pipe cleaner. Totally
antennas on a spacesuit, she says.

SPOILER: The baby has been dead two years now.

The project to convert the dead baby's room into outer space has
been under construction since she was six months pregnant. I
come home one day to find tinfoil satellites strung from the ceiling,
stolen rocks plucked from the neighbor's yard posing as meteors,
a bathtub full of Styrofoam balls - one for each planet + an
enormous sun. Spray cans and cardboard for stenciling.
Space is peaceful, she explains. That night she begins painting the
room black.

≈

According to Einstein, time is just an illusion. Following disaster all
moments begin to bleed together. Linearity becomes inane.

≈

I swear the pale stars seem paler inside this room every day.

As big as space is, the universe inside this little room is rapidly expanding, not contracting. At the rate my wife is filling it with cosmic apparatus it will swallow the entire house like a black hole. The other rooms in the house have gone untouched for quite some time.

Stephen Hawking should've prepared us for this.

≈

We have become aliens.

≈

I place the doll face-down in a field only to pick it back up again. Something about it being smothered in the dark. Ants crawl upon the face, so I wipe them off. I end up hiding it in the basement.

It hits me: I can't let go either.

≈

Three days before the due date she is giving me a tour of the galaxy. She points out several constellations, using my finger to connect them as she explains their mythologies. She indicates the Milky Way, a number of nebulae and other bright asteroid belts. She is proud of her creation. Stifling laughter, she tells me to look through a jumbo telescope with a big red bow on it. See it yet?

I do not.

Upset I'm spoiling her surprise, she grabs my head and drags my skull in front of it. Squint! she orders me. Here we are, she says, pointing to a petite space station smashed between Ursa Minor and a white dwarf. Inside an observation window, two stick people wave out. I'm the one with the big head, she informs me.

≈

The inflationary theory of cosmology suggests the existence of parallel universes like our own but separate in that every possibility that can occur will occur, determining an infinite number of alternate realities. Given the presupposition that the universe is infinite, all realities are equally valid.

≈

There are some complications, says the doctor.

≈

A forgotten Post-it note at the bottom of a closet includes names we'll never have a use for. Now we just call the dead baby NASA.

≈

I have ordered for my wife a lifelike baby doll designed to aid in the grieving process. She is painting a papier-mâché rocket the day the UPS man drops the doll off at the door. I leave it unopened on the kitchen table. I won't open it. I'll just let her discover it, see how she reacts.

Over the weekend it sits there, unperturbed, but on a Sunday evening I find the packaging has been placed in the trash bin. I find H in the backyard, a plastic boy swaddled in her arms. She shhh's me. He's sleeping, she whispers.

That night she places the doll into the crib.

≈

Good grief, a boy in the lab says upon smashing his finger in a doorway.

Don't say that, I tell him. There's no such thing as good grief.

≈

We have become full of black holes.

≈

Bare feet pressed against the glove compartment on our last getaway before parenthood, she smiles as I pretend to guillotine her fingers in the window. I could never live in the desert, she says.

David Bowie is asking me if there is life on Mars. I am asking him
if there is life on Earth.

The rubble of a smashed telescope bought for our son lay
strewn on the patio. My hand is cut. I can't feel it but I know it's
cut because there is proof of my pain on the blood-splashed
pavement. External verification helps, keeps us in check, letting us
know what's real and what's wishful living.

My wife remains in the passenger seat, seatbelt fastened.
Emergency brake lights blink.

I have given my wife an ultimatum: get help or else.

I come home early from work one day to find H standing not more
than four inches from the television. It is the end of *2001: A Space
Odyssey* and she is weeping, her fingers pressed against the glass.
A baby floats in space. She thinks is the most beautiful thing she's
ever seen.

That would be a nice reality . . . but it's not ours, I tell her.

She pretends not to hear this part.

$$\approx$$

Tonight H has been making origami scorpions. Sprawled on the kitchen floor, she folds her one hundredth paper critter and places it on a spilling-over pile. Every day I check on her, every week bringing groceries, making sure she eats something. Whenever I open a cabinet, sand pours out. I offer to make her a *sand*wich, trying for a lame joke. She doesn't laugh.

The project to convert the dead baby's room into a desert has been under construction since the divorce. Now the room has spread into the entire house. There is dust everywhere, glued to the walls, in the seat of the rocking chair, coating sinks. I sweep up what I can. When I walk past the nursery-that-never-was, a fake cactus twinkles Christmas lights at me, a dirt-caked doll tangled in its web. I flip the switch.

On my way out, she says her daily sentence: The desert is romantic, don't you think?

No, I tell her. It's not.

$$\approx$$

The baby choked inside the incubator. The baby choked on air, as one would in space. We have never spoken of the strangeness of this coincidence. Perhaps it's symbolic of something, but of what? I'm no psychologist, just a husband. She won't see a psychologist.

I'm not crazy, she maintains. My baby died . . . my baby is dead. Considering that, I am as sane as humanly possible.

She won't see a psychologist.

$$\approx$$

$$dS = \left(\frac{\delta Q}{T}\right)_{int,rev} \qquad (kJ/K)$$

$$\approx$$

So we supernova.

$$\approx$$

I am dodging dishes in the kitchen. She is cursing, calling me a murderer.

Worried I made a mistake—that it was doing more harm than good—I have gotten rid of that doll in the middle of the night. When she grabs the phone to dial 911 to report an emergency, I grab her and hold her until she calms. We need help, I tell her. She is light years away.

I'm scared, but not for my safety. There is an emergency to report.

≈

Occam's Razor: the simplest explanation is usually true.

≈

Here we sit coming up with names for a boy. In alphabetical order: Aaron. Aldous. Becket. Charles. Crispin. Eli. Herbert. Jack. Jaedon. Jonah. Morris. Oliver. Orson. Oscar. Pete. Simon. Wiley. Xander. How will we ever decide? she wonders. When we see his face we'll know.

≈

I have decided I can't take anymore. Inside, she waits.

I remain in the driver's seat, seatbelt fastened. Emergency brake lights blink.

≈

A funeral, the tiniest coffin I've ever seen and John Lennon singing *Love is real / Real is love.*

≈

In the corner of the room there are new cans now. Colors that have no business in space. My wife, clutching a receipt, waits for me.

We need help, she is willing to admit for the first time.

Are you going to leave me now? she asks, chin twitching, eyes glistening fearful as she floats alone in the center of the room, as she floats alone in an artificial cosmos, walls threatening to swallow her, light painting spiders in her hair, floor wobbling underfoot.

I meet her there.

Wordless, we pry the paint lids. Together we dip a brush, then drag it. We white out the earth first, then each subsequent planet. Make the sun disappear, then kill off the stars. But when it comes to the space station, we pause.

Here we are, I tell her.

REVIVAL

Roxy in the acid jacket wants to bang David Lynch more than she wants to bang me. She admits this to me freely as we cross the overpass right before she points out how funny it would be to kick a dummy over the edge and watch the ensuing panic. I tell her it wouldn't be that funny. She can't hear me over her own laughter.

This girl that I call mine, who wears razorblade scarves and shriveled blue lipstick and high heels with wolf fur that clack incessantly down the boulevard, really belongs to no one. We met three weeks ago at a rare books convention, if you can believe that. I had obtained a pristine first edition of *Ask the Dust*. She cleaved to a battered copy of *The Beautiful and Damned*. I said hello. She asked me to hold her stolen book. A minute later I watched her being patted down and escorted into the foyer while she drunkenly sang out *Happiness is a warm cunt, oh yes it is*! her blue hair bobbing over the crowd.

My pal Jeremy tells me I have a thing for damaged women. He feels I try to save them all, calls it Shining Knight Syndrome. "You can't save nobody that doesn't care enough to save themselves, brother," he tells me. Jeremy was best man at my wedding. He spoke at my wife and kids' funeral.

Right now Roxy and I are walking to the rundown theater that plays older movies on the edge of town. Each month they play a classic. This month it's *To Kill a Mockingbird*.

Roxy says she walks everywhere because she loves the sound of traffic and she really loves the sound of a good car crash, and this city is great because they happen all the time here. I know this to be true from experience. The thing about Roxy is that whenever it gets too quiet, she gets weird and starts talking nonsense. Anytime a casual lull threatens to choke the noise, she says she feels suffocated, like an invisible blanket is smothering her. She begins to ramble. Slowly but surely I'm growing accustomed to these little storms before the silence.

At the theater, we sit waiting for the film to start. It's the middle of the day so it's only us. Roxy spears the silence by saying something about wanting to be baptized in the filth and tears of her ex-lovers. "That's nice," I tell her. She wants to get lit and fuck on a carousel revolving counterclockwise. "You don't say?" She wants to smash butterflies with a ball-peen hammer and hold a revival in the desert to crucify all the believers of Yesterday, whatever the hell this means. "Knock yourself out," I say until the conversation peters out. She throws popcorn until the surround sound kicks in and the trailers roll. She can't stay still for very long. Always has to have something to do with her hands. Motion puts her at ease.

During the dog shooting scene Roxy roots for the dog. She becomes enraged when Atticus puts it down. In the dark I see her spit, her tarantula eye lashes furrow and her tomahawk gaze burn holes into the screen. While Atticus cradles Scout on the bench, I feel Roxy's hand grope inside my pants. This is not the first hand job she has initiated in a public place. She has a fetish for this sort of thing—making love in public, though she hates when I refer to it as "making love." *Making love. No, it's fucking, alright? Get it right.* If this wasn't bad enough, she has this clown nose she carries around in her pocket. If you object to her sexual advances, she stuffs it in your mouth. *Shhhhh. There's a good boy.*

In the few weeks we've been together, we've had sex in every room of her apartment except the bedroom. The bedroom is strictly off limits for sex. The rest of the place is a mess but her bedroom is always spick-and-span, pastel baby blue like a new nursery and littered with stuffed animals, dolls, and snow globes that look like they haven't seen a decent snow for forty winters. I've never asked why the bedroom is off limits. There are other questions I've never asked, too, like how every hanger in the closet came to be twisted, why there are more than twenty phone books strewn throughout the living room, why all her family pictures are hung upside-down on the walls. Our relationship is such that we don't ask these kinds of questions. This arrangement benefits us both.

She is wielding a hot glue gun when I come home from work one afternoon. I watch over her shoulder while she attaches a doll's plucked out limbs back upon the body in grotesque ways: a leg in an arm socket here, an arm sprouting from a torso there. I ask her what she's doing. "Making it beautiful," she says, then something I don't understand about how easily pretty things break, whether their being pretty makes them easy to break or their being easy to break makes them pretty.

That night I am awoken by a timpani clank. I find her in the living room extinguishing a pile of burning dolls. "Call me Ravager," she says. "Ok, Ravager," I say, "you probably shouldn't play with fire in an apartment complex." After she tells me I can suck her dick, she tells me she's going for a ride. I invite myself along for fear of what she'll do in this emotional state.

After careening nowhere in particular through cul-de-sacs and parking lots, we end up in the suburbs and she points out the house in which she grew up. "Doesn't it look like a big dollhouse?" she asks me. It actually does. I can see people through the window and I wonder for a moment if they're dolls pretending to be real people.

"I don't know, man. People are weird when they're in pain," Jeremy tells me over the phone after I've told him of the doll inferno incident. "Sounds like a hot mess to me." I've always confided in Jeremy because he's always been right, but today I resent his wisdom. The resentment burns deep like acid in my stomach. "You can't save people like that." I know he's hinting I should drop Roxy because I'll never be able to save her from herself. What he doesn't understand is that I'm not the knight, I'm the dragon. I have been for some time now. At this point, I've devoured too many princesses to keep count, and I don't care to remember most of their names. I only remember Roxy because she's got my wife's eyes. I don't know what to call that syndrome. All I know is that nobody ever talks about who will save the dragon. In the end, who cares enough to save the dragon?

For weeks now I've been taking Roxy to the dollhouse she grew up in. Sometimes we just watch the people inside from a safe distance, but sometimes we hop the gate and make love in the backyard. Excuse me, we don't "make love," we *fuck*. In fact, I'm not allowed to say make love anymore. It's a small price to pay for being happy. In between the murderous shrieks and squeals, I hear Roxy mutter the only three words that matter concealed under heaving pigbreath. *Louder*, I command her. "I said I love you, punkbitch!" she snarls with gnashing teeth, then wallops me twice over the head with balled fists, digs those wolverine nails of hers into my back, orders me to go deeper. I look around, check to make sure the dolls aren't watching as we sink down behind the swing set in their backyard.

I can hear loose bolts, happy years of play having stressed the parts into a sad state of disrepair. The sun seared leather seat sags low, flirting with the dirt. Paint peels, metal rankles, earth loosens round the anchoring legs. A few warped chinks in the chain are little more than interlocked pinkies. Someday soon it'll all come apart. Someday it'll fold in on itself like a collapsible caravan in the dry mouth of the desert. Someday, but not today. It taunts me, sings a song of rust lurching slow like an apocalypse machine.

Love you too, I tell Roxy before she jams the big red clown nose in my mouth. There are tears becoming lost between us, swallowed and smashed between layers of unholy contour and frantic flapping skin. We do not mention from where they come. We do not speak of these things.

I go deep.

BIOGRAPHY

He prefers stories with climactic endings. Of all the inevitable things—death, taxes, whatever, the one thing he will never not do is say *You, too*! after the lady at the ticket box rips his ticket and tells him to enjoy his film. As a boy he would shovel quarters into novelty machines. At home, he would throw away the contents and admire his vast collection of plastic multicolored bubbles. All ten digits shooting off his hands like blaring rockets and anti-gravity zombies floating through space until they pin him against a Russian satellite and feast in death-silence on his icy organs: to this day, this is the most terrifying dream he's ever had. He feels threatened by the girlfriend who enjoys artificial watermelon flavoring but hates watermelon. Years later, in the throes of withdrawal, he learns in some obscure textbook that love is nothing more than a chemical cocktail, misfit burst of neurons firing, the experience of falling in love no different from a needle full of junk, according to Dr. So-and-So—both addicting as hell and entailing nightmarish comedowns, so that the more a person falls in love the less powerful the high becomes over time, causing one to chase their fix from one dealer to the next trying to recapture that precious first high and doomed to disappointment, since nothing ever beats your first high. Scientists who knew their shit had verified this in experiments. He had verified it in his own unofficial fieldwork. All of us are junkies, he concludes, but just like in the real world only a few of us get to be dealers. His hurried commute through traffic every day is a futile endeavor. If only he stayed in one lane, he would arrive at his destination at precisely the same time. He knows this, but the illusion of progress gives him comfort. Movement trumps stillness. At the age of seven, he slept beneath his bed for fear of what waited for him underneath his sheets. "You got it all wrong," his best friend at the time tried to break it down. "It's the other way around." That was the end of their friendship. Who is anybody to tell us our conception of Heaven, Hell, or The Boogieman? He's always feared his mother's claw foot bath tub, its rusty zigzag smile. Peanut butter makes him claustrophobic—the texture, not the taste. Once in Prague, he was born again, found divinity in the architecture, a righteous curve in every edge. Once in Prague, a gypsy broke a bottle over his skull and borrowed his wallet. Back home in the States, he is quick to kick the windshield out after a car crash, having watched one too many movies, convinced all cars must blow up no matter how serious or minor the collision. Clambering up a hill and scrambling to a safe distance, he plugs his ears and waits for the explosion . . .

POSTLUDE SIX

There is the story of the dress which when worn by her would enrapture all gentlemen callers but at a price, the phantom fabric pulling tighter by the stitch with each kiss. The story of the collar caving in on her larynx, the sleeves swallowing her wrists, the skirt squashing her femur to a fine dust to be pinched between an ex-lover's index and thumb, hemmed by his jealous hands. The story of him attempting to burn the dress in the ravine, the garment's ghost slipping into his gloves, reaching for a lighter and starting at his toes. The story of the folly of fire: how it spreads with ease agitated by the kerosene of envy.

BESTIARY

Some doors once opened can never be closed, but we can choose to avoid those rooms that are bad for us. Long before she suffers the meaning of his favorite mantra, the one Dr. Pratz dispenses like miracle pills to patients of Red Ward because it emphasizes the triumph of choice and self-restraint over man's basest impulses, Hazeline realizes her singular gift from the fairy tales her father tells her—for when Little Red Riding Hood embarks to grandmother's house she finds that all her sympathy falls instead to the Big Bad Wolf, who in her heart she truly believes had not been born a monster.

From an early age she senses this makes her strange. It's unnatural, somehow a sin to feel more for the villain, whose presence is manufactured by the writer to root against with ease. Deep down in the marrow of her bones, twitching in her gut, she suspects there may fester the seed of something more sinister. To empathize with beasts where other children know the automatic difference between right and wrong, light and darkness, serpents and lambs, is vile.   *So I'll be vile*, she decides.

In other words, she knows she is broken. She tells no one of her brokenness. In a princess-pink room she nurses it, poring through storybooks in an artificial cave of serrated shadows and sheet creases until the flashlight flickers and dies. Graffitis margins with alternate endings so the itsy bitsy spider escapes the wrath of the rain, the evil Djinn isn't imprisoned in a bottle therefore doesn't inherit his murderous rage, and so Rumpelstiltskin eventually comes to love the first-born child, giving it back to the miller's daughter upon witnessing from the shadows the depths of her grief.

This is how her fascination begins.

The Bestiary is born on a napkin in a high school cafeteria. Young Hazeline sits alone, kneecaps crushed tightly together, scratching names of the top ten misunderstood antagonists, unable to touch food on her tray she is in such a frenzy. By college it is a full-fledged obsession, her dorm littered with colored notecards spilling out of cabinets: a private compendium of fiends from pop culture, cinema, fairy tales and folklore. By grad school, she is on her way to a doctorate of deviant psychology, dedicated to redeeming the irredeemable.

Red Ward, so named for the ketchup-colored doors along the main corridor of the facility, painted in 1989 by order of Dr. Sevarou, who believes red to be the color of passion and that sexual offenders ought at all times be reminded of their crimes. These days, though, things are different. Rehabilitation is the word. Visitors are no longer referred to as offenders—they are patients. They have an illness. They're sick. In the spring of 2004 all the red doors are repainted blue, the color designated by Dr. Pratz for its symbolism: purity, calm, water as a great cosmic cleansing force.

In a familiar cinematic scene, a mob gathers outside a village clinking pitchforks and waving torches all too eager to hunt The Wolfman. It is not his lupine form they fear but the fact that he spends half his time like them - among them - and it is nearly impossible to distinguish where one form ends and the other begins.

Something she has never forgotten, seared into her memory: Rufus the dog has latched on to the neighbor's birds and is shaking them something fierce, painting red the patio, fleecing feathers through the yard. *What's wrong with him?* Hazeline wants to know, but Father is walking away now, slipping into the garage and searching for his shovel. When he returns he finds a yard without a dog, the fence door having been flung open.

A slightly obscure tale: a princess is held captive by a blind dragon. When a brave knight appears at the mouth of the cave to slay her captor, he is turned away by the princess. What a lonely beast this one must be, she answers when the knight demands a reason. There she remains until the end of her days.

Some days it is not so bad. Mirrors don't blacken, bend under the weight of a breath. Gravity holds. Leonard feels his feet firmly grafted to the earth. Other days, the chandelier swarms with snakes. Like sleeping through a lattice of ghost nets. Like keeping your goodbyes in a glass case. Like the sun full of black snow. Days like these, a circle could kill.

Sol smiles stupid handing out treasure maps during another group session, which patients take turns leading weekly. Where 'X' marks the spot the word Peace is embossed in blue, a dotted trail fraught with 12 steps of self-scrutiny winding across the damaged landscape with bulleted tips like Limit Your Masturbation - Remove Yourself From The Wrong Situation - Know Your Triggers - Et cetera Et cetera. Above a golden compass in holy cursive: *Time heals all wounds.* Folding the page 12 times, Leonard thinks: *We don't need your dark map to remind us no two wounds are alike…we don't need your dark map to remind us all wounds are the same.*

Like a person, you can fold a page only so many times until it is no longer capable of folding.

If anything, time exhumes all wounds, resurrects them, stirs the dirt to make them fresh again.

To deny this is as ridiculous as attempting to bury the sky.

"Perhaps everything terrible is in its deepest being something helpless that wants help from us."

Over her desk is pinned the quote which (the night she got the call that her Father's skull filled with blood, an unimpeachable joy rippled through her, causing fat droplets to plink upon the page) scratched itself upon her heart.

Even Satan, the original villain, isn't beyond a soft spot. For if Paradise were truly Paradise, how could an angel be so broken?

What about it scares you? Hazeline asks to kick off the session.

The way it never ends. Like the idea of infinity. Terrifying, Leonard answers.

When she draws an enormous circle on the blackboard behind her, Leonard shuffles in his seat. When she draws another he becomes visibly agitated.

How do you feel now?

Unsafe.

You're safe. I promise you.

When she draws a third circle interpenetrating the others, Leonard stands up, his fists balled.

Erase them, he tells her. Now.

She does.

Now tell me how that made you feel...

Later, Hazeline is willing to admit to herself how scared she was. Here at Red Ward it is Leonard, at twenty-three the youngest and most volatile patient, that has only ever made her fear like that. From that day onward, a muscle man is always outside her door during sessions.

T rypophobia: fear of circles, as in, fear of holes, tightly clustered, as in, a wasp nest or honeycomb or sponge, as in, the fear of falling through.

Frankenstein's monster didn't choose to be Frankenstein's monster.

They all have their hobbies during the late afternoon hours. Terry, a connoisseur of classics like Pac-Man and Pong, can be heard cursing his video games all the way from check-in. Sol contents himself tinkering with his wrist watch, tightening tiny springs, or his model carnival clicking together plastic Ferris wheels or painting petite clowns – it is the most difficult thing in the world to get their red noses right. Leonard, meanwhile, ignores concentric cracks in the library's linoleum deriving his salvation from stories. Here, it is important to have a hobby. Something, anything to do with your hands.

A little icon blinks across a blueblack grid chasing ghosts and the occasional cherry. But there is a fatal flaw in the design: the game is glitched, never-ending, rigged for infinite loop. Some master programmer's cruel ploy to suck quarters of young boys, also known as a kill screen.

Jack be nimble, Jack be quick, but Jack couldn't resist the allure of candlesticks.

For this next exercise, they're told to write 'It's not your fault' in the center of the page, but Leonard's first impulse is to make it smaller, so he erases it and makes it smaller, then scratches it out before erasing it altogether. When Dr. Pratz asks him why he did it, he tells the truth: Because it doesn't work like that. Because it's only ink on paper. Because deep down, he knows he should've been smarter, stronger, more fortified. Because maybe he deserved it. Because through the palimpsest all he makes out is 'It's your fault' and this tiny piece of paper could never be big enough.

Not by the hair of my chinny chin chin! says Pig #1. Years later, it is not the wolf heaving at his door that haunts him but the shame of having built his house with straw.

On the subject of villains who are their own worst enemy, Dr. Jekyll and Mr. Hyde is an obvious example. More complicated though is the saga of Gilgamesh, a tyrannical king who, when he met the wild man Enkidu was tamed by companionship. But upon encountering the giant Humbaba in the cedar forest, it was Enkidu who urged Gilgamesh to abandon mercy, slaying him on the forest floor in spite of his begging.

Some days Leonard suspects Rhea is a plant – other days he is sure of it. Shiny bear trap waiting to snag ankles with a rusty snap-clang. Why else would they hire an RN like her? With her pixie haircut and boyish face, she could pass for twelve, thirteen. This is something Dr. Sevarou would've concocted to keep the freaks in check, but not Dr. Pratz. This is a dangerous place for her. Oblivious she goes about her work, and where she goes he memorizes, until he knows her routine like the back of his hand.

Sometimes Hazeline wants to touch her patients – those who need it most, for whom touch has been perverted. Sol sits weeping on an orange bench, his application for housing having been denied for the 16th month in a row. Ordered out by Judge Pritchard, all that has stood between his release from Red Ward is the community placement agreement: that little slip of paper granting him another shot at life in the outside world. *I'll never have a place, will I?* he says softly. Makes his peace with it, fidgeting with his watch. Then: *Does such a place even exist?* His hands catch his face as he continues to sob. Hazeline scoots closer in her rolling chair. What he says isn't rhetorical. Everyone everywhere believes in the capacity for change, just not in *their* immediate neighborhood. In the end, she settles for therapeutic jargon, backing away, assuming once again a professional distance. *Next month*, she says. It's a good answer. Sol smiles, knowing the drill. Thank you, he says. He means it. How she tries. *Next month*. It's a lie, but a kind lie at least.

Often considered a hero, The Pied Piper is well known for leading all the rats out of Hamelin with his magic flute. But when they refused to pay him for his services, he led all the children of the town to the river, where with unpardonable glee he watched them drown.

Crawling into the doghouse, Young Hazeline hides. Tucks her knees safe inside with the stink of warm fur and ragdoll chew toys making her mouth into a zipper: partially to delay her impending lesson, partially to preen for the lashing.

Leonard sits wedged behind a half table, palms up, watching grainy video of children splashing in a kiddy pool. As they slap small waves his hands begin to tremble, his chin lowers, sunken in shame. The PCI blinks, triggering the screen to switch back to normative stimuli: a hummingbird ascending in slow motion, whittling its path through the rain with a delicate fury of wingbeats. Leonard, moved by this, curves his cap to conceal his face. No matter how small the creature, what a burden to carry this terrible weight we've been given. Through a pane Rhea jots down the results. Like a tornado torn in half forced to unveil its frightening symmetry, eerie it is how much like stillness the slow spin of some catastrophes.

Castration is a last resort, Dr. Pratz explains to Leonard again. Every week he asks a white coat to sign off on the procedure. Every week he says he's ready. Every week he is turned down.

And all the king's horses and all the king's men couldn't put Humpty together again.

It is a ritual for Dr. Pratz to turn off Hazeline's computer, which she leaves on more often than not, fond of getting lost in Wikipedia's vortex on her lunch break. Most of the time he doesn't read the screen – it's none of his business, after all – but today he does, dismayed by the icy gorgon's gaze:

> In a late version of the Medusa myth, related by the Roman poet Ovid (Metamorphoses 4.770), Medusa was originally a ravishingly beautiful maiden, 'the jealous aspiration of many suitors,' but when she was caught being raped by the 'Lord of the Sea' Poseidon in Athena's temple, the enraged Athena transformed Medusa's beautiful hair to serpents and made her face so terrible to behold that the mere sight of it would turn onlookers to stone. In Ovid's telling, Perseus describes Medusa's punishment by Minerva (Athena) as just and well earned.

There was once a patient who came through with a bevy of birds in tow. There was once a patient who came back from lunch to find his birds missing, all the little latches sprung, window open. Nothing against birds… it was the cages Leonard hated.

In the courtyard, Leonard sits fumbling with the bill of his cap and rustling earmarked pages of his favorite book, The Count of Monte Cristo. He has read it six times now, almost seven, with quite a few passages memorized, queued up in his mind like misfit prayers to some obscure god. His second most earmarked book, A Wonder-Book for Girls and Boys by Nathaniel Hawthorne, is a close second though, because of its inclusion of his favorite story *The Paradise of Children*, in which kids are briefly described as living happily alone in a world without adults.

"For all evils there are two remedies - time and silence."

–Alexandre Dumas

Captain Hook can feel his phantom hand at night. Tosses and turns with the swaying of the ship. Hears the ticking of clocks long since smashed. No one suspects once upon a time he too was a lost boy.

Where the narrow halls separate like chambers of a heart, every blue door stands wide open now as festive music floats from the cafeteria. It is the annual New Year's Party and Sol is folding his accordion, playing for the fourth time the only tune he knows. Terry with the brigadier mustache and giant spatula hands pours a second bag of sugar into the punch, yowls upon sipping the ladle. When the white coats turn their head he empties in a tin flask. He will be the one to distribute refreshments throughout the evening, and only once will somebody make a crack about how fitting it is considering his history of date rape. Only once, because he'll snap then, flinging the ladle across the room and kicking the cooler to the floor, charging forth with a plastic fork. Before the muscle men arrive he will have already apologized, more embarrassed than anything else, his ridiculer having apologized too, extending a hand to acknowledge his cardinal sin: in a place where everyone is equally guilty, no one proud of what they did or what they are, it is cruelty to wave someone's past in front of his face. No one is in need of a history lesson when every morning is a brand new martyrdom. Forced to attend, Leonard sits in a corner folding a paper horn in half, watching Rhea through a cloud of confetti as Sol offers her his tinsel tiara. She accepts, placing it crooked on her head like a queen of small slaughters.

Under permahiss of powerlines, Hazeline stands watching a snagged kite sizzle overhead. Whips its tail once, twice, before slipping from the sagging wire to the sidewalk below.

Some doors, once opened, can never be closed but we can choose to avoid those rooms that are bad for us. Unless you're the house in the metaphor. Soon that room bleeds out into the hallway infecting your floors, which threaten to give way with each footfall, and your walls which, with their pained joints of abuse sway assailed by windlash and the chronic gnaw of rats… then creeping up the spiral stairs to your attic and down to your basement below, invading like a slow pestilence - like hungry ghosts shooting tendrils from the mouth, wearing their theft-of-night like tourniquets - until no room of you is left spared and outside every window a heart hangs impaled upon the moon.

Having deconstructed the house metaphor enough to prove it futile, Leonard sits twiddling his fingers and watching Rhea through an amber pane, sun-sloshed so as to resemble an angel swimming through a jar of formaldehyde.

The Minotaur doesn't understand why he's been imprisoned in the Labyrinth any more than we do. It is unknown whether or not he would leave if given the opportunity, but it is a moot point: he will never be given the opportunity, for he is the Minotaur and the Labyrinth is his home.

Out of the corner of Leonard's eye, Rhea with a snapped tiara can be seen escorting Sol to his room with a cup in each hand, hiccupping - *Auld Lang Syne* -

Sometimes the carpet is lava, so Young Leonard uses a pair
of pillows to navigate the hallway. If his toes touch even a fiber
he knows they'll burn clean off. He takes his time switching out
pillows, steadying himself, inhale-hop-exhale, until he is safely over
tile in the kitchen. Later, face down on the floor he'll notice the
mosaic design that resembles pennies impinging pennies, a virus of
Venn diagrams that never end, like pores on a pair of cold hands
that wring an unsuspecting neck from behind.

When Hazeline opens the door she flicks on the light to see Rhea crumpled in the corner, clutching in her hands a well-worn gray cap, shattered tiara bits by her knees on a splash of red. Plastic diamonds litter the floor. At first tripping on her words while Hazeline yells into the hall, eventually Rhea summons speech. Leonard: the name crackles up through her throat. Hazeline is quick to report his name through a phone she has yanked from a nearby wall. —helped me. Saved me, Rhea finally finishes her sentence, folding her knees up now and tucking the faded cap under her chin. Fake diamonds flash like the real thing under cheap florescence.

The janitor opens the closet to find the body that has been dragged there out of panic, pants twisted around its ankles, bare torso black and blue. Calls out twice before he recognizes the watch.

At age seven, Young Leonard leaves his closet door cracked, convinced by now it is the monsters outside the closet he should fear.

"His mind was filled with a single thought: that of his happiness destroyed for no apparent reason."

—Alexandre Dumas

Hazeline finds him fetal on the ground in his quarters, halfway under his bunk, babbling. When she lies down beside him he is slow to turn. He looks so different without his cap. Face sogged, fists bloodied, he is perfumed in shame, his face is not the face of a man but the immutable face of a boy, forever nervous, forever afraid of himself and the world around him. His babbling unravels: *he was hurting her...*   Taking hold of him the way her mother took hold of her the day she told her the news, he continues to try and speak, as though he is choked on needles it is so painful to expel those words. So she hushes him, holding tight, tighter, tighter still, until all language is obliterated, their clumsy alphabets swallowed by the sound of sirens coming to sing the long, indissoluble night into passing.

In an alternate version of the story, the Big Bad Wolf catches his reflection in a mirror before Little Red Riding Hood's arrival, and seeing himself for what he truly is proceeds to bite his tail off before prying out his canines with a rusty letter opener. Moral: A wolf is a wolf is a wolf.

Another version posits a reversal of roles: It is not Little Red Riding Hood but the Big Bad Wolf on his way to his grandmother's house. When he arrives at her cave he finds a girl dressed in the fur of his grandmother, milkwhite teeth smeared rouge - the girl having been taught early on the wickedness of wolves by her father the hunter. Moral: A wolf is a wolf is still a wolf, but only because the woods made it that way.

In yet another variation, Little Red Riding Hood never makes it to grandmother's house, becoming lost in the woods and remaining lost forever. Sleeping upon twigs she learns to live among the animals, though she never stops fearing night and all that night stands for. The Big Bad Wolf, equally afraid of the forest floor, climbs a tree one morning and vows never to come down until he is transformed into a human man by Mother Moon. When Little Red Riding Hood comes upon the beast having thrown himself from the top of the tallest tree, she buries him, wrapping him in her red cloak and placing bright flowers upon his grave and that is all.

Though they had never met, she senses they've known each other all their lives.

POSTLUDE SEVEN

There is the story of the window which every so often would flash with the glimpse of his near future, but only ten minutes ahead. The story of the man addicted to watching the window for any sign of distress, any forewarning that would spare him the fate of all men. The story of his losing everything over his obsession, his job, his children, his marriage, his mind. The story of the brick thrown by a heartbroken bride. The story of a delicious shattering, an arabesque of beautiful emergency. The story of joy in never knowing the ukulele logic of tomorrow.

INTERACTIVE MISCELLANEA & EPHEMERA

The following is a list of digital works by the author:

IN SEARCH OF: A SANDBOX NOVEL
http://www.insearchofthenovel.com

BESTIARY
http://willock77.wix.com/bestiary

WRITER: THE GAME
http://willock77.wix.com/writerthegame

ARE YOU THERE, INTERNET? IT'S ME, BOLIVIA
http://willock77.wix.com/areyouthereinternet

ADJUNCT: A SURVIVAL HORROR ADVENTURE
http://writer.inklestudios.com/stories/h6b8

TOTIDEM VERBIS
http://writer.inklestudios.com/stories/45gr

THANK YOU

If this book could talk, after screaming it would babble plentiful thank yous to a vast configuration of kind hearts in the literary community for allowing me a tiny voice in this love-sogged landscape of endless talent and artistic integrity, particularly KERNPUNKT Press, Passenger Side Books, Red Bird Chapbooks, Permafrost, PANK, Best American Experimental Writing, and BOAAT press.

—————————————————

If this book could talk, after screaming and babbling plentiful thank yous it would yodel a secret song for Van Choojitarom, Alisha Karabinus, Clarinda D'Cruze, Nathan Blake, Jake Syersak, Silas Hansen, Abby Norwood, Kat Finch, Portia Elan, Kaushik Viswanath, Xin Tian, Kallie Rose, Jill Kolongowski, Jane Childs, Fatima Z. Ahmed, Katie O, Meg Freitag, Megan Pillow Davis, Emily Rose Cole, Ryan Werner, Kia Alice Groom, Mimi Lipson, Sean Shearer, Kat Lewin, Molly Gaudry, Sam Snoek-Brown, Michael Martin Shea, Cody Klippenstein, Amy Rossi, Anita B, all the Bens, Aaron Teel, Garrard Conley, Samuel Hovda, Dini Parayitam, Garth Greenwell, Jamel Brinkley, Jeremy Kinser, Martha Pierce, Kevin Brockmeier, Lan Samantha Chang, Daniel Orozco, Amos Magliocco, Barbara Rodman, and Steve Buscemi.

—————————————————

If this book could talk, after screaming and babbling plentiful thank yous and yodeling a secret song it would then say a psalm of extra special gratitude to my family – mom, dad, Kevin, Bonnie, Kylie, and Ginger - for their boundless support, my wife Heather (I promise to finish your YA book now!), and Tinna the cosmic dachshund.

Finally, if this book could talk, after screaming and babbling plentiful thank yous and yodeling a secret song and saying a psalm of extra special gratitude, it would stretch forth its neon tongue and tickle the dappled ether that is YOU: its dear reader.

Sincerely,

M

Note from the Author (On Wizardry)

At its worst, writing is a lonely grisly business. Putting words on a page always sounds simple until you realize it's like trying to unearth a splinter lodged square in your soul. You pick and you pick and sometimes you get close but nothing really ever rids you of that sucker. The truth is, you grow fond of the picking. The ceaseless poking and prodding, yet the twinge and terror of that soul shrapnel is omnipresent and ever-haunting. Some would like to think it a noble undertaking, but if there's anything noble about it it's only your eventual embrace of some Sisyphean addiction. At its best though, writing is the closest thing we have to real wizardry, enabling a direct connection between total strangers that is somehow able to bypass all the bullshit and barriers that typically prevent us from treating each other like decent human beings when we're trapped inside our skinsuits. Somehow, existing pure on the page, unfiltered and unfettered, we are finally free to dare to know one another. All pretense dropped, a bridge of ink stretches forth through the void and invites two perfect strangers to stand feasting together upon the same beatific or terrible, ecstatic truths. When it's over, the book closing, the bridge folds up and all go home, but that singular moment of shared suffering on the bridge remains and is never lost, not really. It either leaves its mark somewhere in the dingy ductwork of imagination, or warmly tattoos itself where only the most sacred things preside—our most exalted heart-scars.